Help the Herd

by Carol Domblewski
illustrated by Donald Cook

HOUGHTON MIFFLIN   BOSTON

In southern Montana, a few miles away from the Yellowstone River, lies a small spread called the Double H Ranch, run by the family of eleven-year-old Trevor Mulligan. They raise sheep and cattle in Big Sky country.

Early one summer morning, Trevor's mom puts him in charge of the sheep. It's one of Trevor's favorite tasks on the ranch.

"Come, Lucky!" Trevor shouts. Far across the field, a black-and-white dog looks up and, without hesitating for a second, races in the direction of Trevor's voice. A minute later, Lucky is by Trevor's side. She is wagging her tail and jumping excitedly all around him.

Lucky is Trevor's three-year-old Border collie and one of the family dogs, but she is much more than a pet. She is also an important worker on the Double H Ranch.

With Lucky at his side, Trevor opens the sheep pen, which contains sixty-three sheep, but the sheep don't come out yet. There is just one dog to herd them all, but Trevor is not a bit worried. He knows that Lucky is just the dog for the job. She is smart and gentle with the sheep, but she can also command them, just as Trevor can command her.

Trevor begins walking toward a nearby field, where the sheep will graze today. But Lucky does not move. From the sheep pen she watches Trevor as carefully as she would watch a butcher slice a steak, and she waits for him to tell her what to do. Today Trevor is Lucky's handler—the person who gives her commands.

When Trevor reaches the grazing area, he turns around and calls loudly to Lucky. "Bring them!" He calls only once, but Lucky springs into action. "Bring them" tells Lucky to take the sheep to Trevor. She now begins to herd the sheep.

All at once, the sheep begin to move. They leave the pen, spreading out in all directions. Trevor knows they should be moved in a tight, orderly circle. "Go by," he calls out to Lucky in a voice that is clear and firm. This tells Lucky to move toward the left of the flock of sheep. As she moves to the left, the sheep on that side begin to draw closer toward the center of the group, and the circle of sheep tightens.

Then Trevor calls in a different tone of voice: "Go away."
This tells Lucky to go right. With lightning speed, Lucky is
on the other side of the flock in an instant. The sheep there
start moving closer to the center of the group, and soon the
flock forms the tight circle Trevor wants. Now the sheep are
all moving toward him, and Lucky is right behind them.

Like her ancestors, Lucky is a great herding dog. Border collies and some other breeds, or types, such as German shepherds and Australian shepherds, are known as sheep-herding dogs. Whether or not they are trained, these dogs have an instinct—a sense they are born with—to run in circles around groups of animals. This was originally a hunting instinct, but centuries of careful breeding have shaped this ability into a way for the dogs to work effectively with humans.

However, it takes more than instinct to make a great sheep herder like Lucky. It takes long hours of training. Trevor's mother taught Lucky her first commands: "come," "sit," "stay," and "down." To help Lucky understand what each command meant, she used a combination of her voice and movements. For example, for the command "sit," she raised the first finger of her hand, lifted it dramatically to her nose, and then brought it down fast and hard. For "down," she bent over and placed her hand on the ground right in front of Lucky's face. She repeated each command in exactly the same tone of voice and with exactly the same movements each time.

Each time Lucky did what she was told, Trevor's mother gave her a reward, such as a small treat. She also used exactly the same praising tone of voice. "Good dog, Lucky," she would say enthusiastically and kindly, and then she patted the dog on the head or stroked her back. However, Trevor's mom never gave the dog any rewards or praise if Lucky did not do exactly the right thing as soon as she heard the command. Soon, Lucky understood what was expected and would always do whatever Trevor's mother commanded, the moment she commanded it.

To learn to herd sheep was harder, however. Lucky had an instinct for herding, but she was still sent to a professional sheep-herding trainer. She needed a professional trainer partly because herding sheep is complicated and requires several different kinds of skills, and partly because there are about thirty herding commands Lucky needed to learn. Each dog also has its own way of herding, called "style." A professional trainer would help Lucky develop her own style of herding.

Sheep-herding dogs don't understand the different words of the many commands they learn. But they do understand the tones of voice in which the commands are given, or the hand signals or whistles that express them.

Today, Trevor will use several of the commands that Lucky has been trained to follow. It turns out that the grazing site he has chosen is not very good. So, with Lucky's help, he needs to move the sheep several miles to a different spot.

It's time for Lucky to "drive" the herd. Driving means moving the sheep away from the handler. Lucky had to receive a lot of training to do this, because the instinct she was born with tells her always to bring the sheep *toward* the handler. Now, however, she will get the sheep to move ahead of Trevor.

As soon as Trevor gives the command for driving, Lucky runs right behind the sheep, barks a little, and makes them move. When Trevor sees that the sheep begin running too fast, he calls, "Take time!" Trevor knows they all have a long distance to go, and he wants Lucky and the sheep to slow down. Hearing the command, Lucky knows she should slow down and also not get too close to the sheep. In an instant, she slows her pace and, at the same time, drops back a little.

Now the entire group—sheep, Trevor, and Lucky—are all moving over the ranch at a slow but steady pace. As they make their way toward the new grazing spot, Trevor gives additional commands to keep the sheep in a tight circle.

At last they reach the pasture Trevor wants to try next. The grazing is much better here than in the previous spot. The sheep settle in and forage on the grasses. Trevor takes out his snack and entrusts the herd to Lucky's watchful eyes. Lucky approaches as Trevor is about to finish, and he gives her some dog treats he has brought in his bag for her.

After a couple of hours, Trevor notices some dark clouds in the distance. Some of the sheep are restless. Lucky picks up on their nervous tension and begins to move from one side of the flock to the other, keeping the group together. Normally sheep don't mind rain, but Trevor fears that a thunderstorm is approaching, and a storm could endanger them all if it brings lightning with it. Lucky is usually good during a storm, but Trevor doesn't want to take any chances.

"Bring them!" Trevor calls to Lucky, and they all begin to head back to the ranch.

At one point on their return, three sheep begin to separate from the flock and start heading toward one of the small tributaries of the Yellowstone River. Wandering like this is dangerous for the sheep, because they could easily get stranded in the water or lost. Predators like wolves or coyotes might even attack them if they wander too far.

But Lucky knows what to do, even without a command. She runs to the side of one of the younger, smaller sheep. It is the baby of one of the larger separated sheep. Lucky gives the young sheep "the eye," another one of the Border collie's skills in herding. This means she looks at the sheep in a way that says, "I'm the boss, and you get back into line right now!" The young sheep hurries back toward the flock, and its mother and the other stray sheep promptly follow.

Trevor, Lucky, and the sheep are about halfway home when another sheep begins to stray from the herd. Trevor gives Lucky the command to bring it back. Lucky runs up very close to the sheep and gives it the eye. This sheep is not so young and not so agreeable as the first one, however. It wavers back and forth, as though it can't make up its mind what to do. So Lucky gets a little tougher; she nudges the sheep with her head, and this does the trick. The sheep rejoins the flock.

Lucky has done harder jobs than this. One of them is called "shedding." Sometimes, one sheep in a flock gets sick and has to be separated from the herd. Because sheep like to stay together, getting that one sheep out of the herd is not easy! A good sheep-herding dog, however, will follow a series of commands to do this work. For a challenging job like this, Lucky might work with a second sheep-herding dog. Together, they will have no trouble getting the job done.

After a long morning, and just as raindrops begin to fall, Trevor commands Lucky to bring the flock back to the pen. Trevor is tired, and the sheep, which have also been expending a lot of energy, are moving much slower than they did earlier. But Lucky is still full of pep. Dogs like her seem to be able to work forever. In fact, her breed, or type, is known as a working dog—a dog that helps people do the work of everyday life.

There are many other kinds of working dogs. Some dogs work in the military, police, or security. Dogs also help people with search-and-rescue operations. In cold climates, sled dogs pull people and goods on sleds. And dogs also guard herds of livestock—a slightly different job than the one Lucky has.

When the sheep are safely back in the pen, Trevor calls Lucky to him one last time. She sits at his feet, wags her tail, and looks up at him with eager eyes. She seems not to notice the rain, which is falling harder now. Trevor crouches down and pets her soft head. Then he scratches her behind the ears, a reward that she loves. He thinks she's the best dog ever—sweet, lively, and intelligent. She's also a hard worker. "Good dog, Lucky!" he says, and he really means it.